THE OFFICIAL

Celtic ANNUAL 2004

Written by
Douglas Russell

g

A Grange Publication

© 2003. Published by Grange Communications Ltd., Edinburgh, under licence from Celtic Football Club. Printed in the EU.

ISBN 1-902704-49-5

CONTENTS

If You Know The History

CELTIC – THE HONOURS

Scottish League Championships (38 in total)

1892/93, 1893/94, 1895/96, 1897/98, 1904/05, 1905/06, 1906/07, 1907/08, 1908/09, 1909/10, 1913/14, 1914/15, 1915/16, 1916/17, 1918/19, 1921/22, 1925/26, 1935/36, 1937/38, 1953/54, 1965/66, 1966/67, 1967/68, 1968/69, 1969/70, 1970/71, 1971/72, 1972/73, 1973/74, 1976/77, 1978/79, 1980/81, 1981/82, 1985/86, 1987/88, 1997/98, 2000/01, 2001/02.

Scottish Cups (31)

1892, 1899, 1900, 1904, 1907, 1908, 1911, 1912, 1914, 1923, 1925, 1927, 1931, 1933, 1937, 1951, 1954, 1965, 1967, 1969, 1971, 1972, 1974, 1975, 1977, 1980, 1985, 1988, 1989, 1995, 2001.

Scottish League Cups (12)

1956, 1957, 1965, 1966, 1967, 1968, 1969, 1974, 1982, 1997, 2000, 2001.

European Cup 1967

UEFA Cup Runners up 2003

Coronation Cup 1953

St. Mungo Cup 1951

Victory in Europe Cup 1945

Empire Exhibition Trophy 1938

Scottish League Commemorative Shield 1904/05 – 1909/10

Glasgow Exhibition Cup 1902

Martin O'Neill

Now in his fourth year with the club, manager Martin O'Neill came so close to European glory in Season 2002/03, after having guided his charges to the final of the UEFA Cup. Amongst others, Blackburn Rovers, Stuttgart and Liverpool were left in his team's shadow on the road to Seville. Although the SPL title was not retained, it was only lost on goal-difference on the last day of the season after Celtic had played 120 minutes of football in 110 degrees heat four days earlier. In truth, his charges had been superb all season and deserved far more than to be runners-up in both the UEFA Cup and the SPL Championship.

Celtic

Robert Douglas

Goalkeeper for both club and country, Douglas made thirty-eight starts in the various domestic and European competitions throughout Season 2002/03. After a double hernia operation last January, he returned to the fray for the February UEFA Cup game with Stuttgart at Celtic Park even although not fully recovered. In the same tournament the previous October, he would just not be beaten by the strikers of Blackburn Rovers in either leg. Fast forward the calendar to March 2003 when Celts travelled to face Liverpool at Anfield following a 1-1 drawn game in Glasgow. With the score still 0-0 in the first-half of that Merseyside clash, Douglas made a superb save from Steven Gerrard's powerful drive before producing another excellent stop, but this time in the second period of play, from the same Premiership pin-up. Two weeks before this five star display, Celtic entertained Rangers in an SPL clash that they just had to win. Once again, Rab more than played his part and, with the team 1-0 ahead courtesy of John Hartson's goal, made a fine save from Amoruso's thundering strike right at the end of the ninety minutes to ensure that all three points remained in the east end of the city. On the international stage, the big man pulled off two remarkable saves from Bernd Schneider (one in each half) when Scotland held World Cup runners-up Germany 1-1 in the crucial European qualifier of early June 2003.

Magnus Hedman

The Swedish international team-mate of both Henrik Larsson and Johan Mjallby, appeared some one hundred and fifty times for Coventry before arriving at Celtic for £1.5 million in the summer of 2002. Hedman then made his debut in the 5-0 Glasgow thrashing of Dundee United in August that same summer but, as was the case with his fellow countryman Mjallby, injury became a key element of his season. Although the keeper ended the 2002/03 campaign with just ten starts to his name, he did appear in eight consecutive league and cup games (which included a total of five clean sheets) from late December's 4-2 victory over Hearts to early February's 2-1 SPL win over Livingston.

Joos Valgaeren

The Belgian-born defender, always comfortable on the ball, was an ever-present in the SPL title campaign until the early April game with Dundee at Dens Park which was drawn 1-1. By season's end in late May 2003, no other Celtic first-team player had bettered his fifty-three home and abroad starts. Equalling his tally of three goals from the previous year, Valgaeren (now in his fourth term at Celtic Park) netted in the UEFA Cup tie with FK Suduva (8-1, 19.9.03) and the SPL clashes with both Motherwell at home (3-1, 1.12.02) and Kilmarnock at Rugby Park (1-1, 15.12.02) during the first-half of Season 2002/03. At Ibrox in late May, when manager Martin O'Neill digressed from his usual 3-5-2 configuration, Joos was quite at home (and superb!) at the centre of a flat back four formation in the vital 2-1 league triumph that blew the league race wide open. Making the victory all the more impressive was the fact that Celtic played this game less than seventy-two hours after their UEFA Cup semi-final with Boavista in Portugal.

Ulrik Laursen

After joining the club from Hibernian in the summer of 2002, the Dane made a solid, confident debut when Celtic hit a high five and sent visitors Dundee United back home to think again that same summertime (5-0, 17.8.02). In all, with fellow Scandinavian Johan Mjallby posted missing through injury, the defender secured a first-team berth thirty-four times last season. When Rangers were beaten 2-1 at Ibrox in late April 2003, Laursen was at his most assured and played supremely well as part of a flat back four that Sunday lunchtime.

With injury, unfortunately, playing a major part in the Swedish defender's 2002/03 Season (Mjallby was absent from the beginning of September until the end of December), it meant that the stopper only began a total of twenty-four league, cup and European games. This was in sharp contrast to the 2001/02 term when he was one of only two Celtic players who made more than fifty appearances for the club that year.

He did however equal his tally of three goals from that period with strikes in the encounters with Aberdeen at Pittodrie (the opener in the 4-0 August rout), Hibernian at Celtic Park (the sensational injury time winner when it looked as if Celts would drop two points but managed to secure all three right at the death in the 3-2 early March victory) and Dundee in the last home game of the season when Jim Duffy's outfit were crushed 6-2. Mjallby often gives the impression that he would do almost anything for the Celtic cause.

David Fernandez

The Spaniard is now in the second of his four year Celtic contract after having arrived at the club from Livingston in the summer of 2002. Fernandez scored his first ever goal for the team back in October last season (a delightful lob over FK Suduva keeper Padimanskas) when the Bhoys travelled to Lithuania on European duty at the very beginning of what would become, in time, a truly joyous UEFA Cup journey lasting several months. The player made the starting line-up a total of eight times during Season 2002/03.

Didier Agathe

With his blistering pace, Didier Agathe in full flight is indeed a sight to behold. Although the player did not score himself in Season 2002/03, his actual 'goal' contribution was important on many occasions throughout that period, especially during Celtic's wonderfully emotional European expedition. When the team travelled to play Bundesliga high-flyers Stuttgart in Germany last February, Agathe's role in the Bhoys two early strikes was crucial. Firstly, he crossed for John Hartson (who headed on for Alan Thompson to score) and, secondly, his pace left defender Wenzel for dead before Chris Sutton benefited in front of goal just a couple of minutes later. After the game, Stuttgart's coach Felix Magath commented that Agathe was international class. In the semi-final of the same tournament, Boavista held the wing-back in such high regard that they detailed not one but two players to track his movements during the first-leg in Glasgow! Of course, in the Seville final some weeks later, his deep penetrating cross early in the second-half of the game led to Henrik Larsson's first equaliser of the night. Didier began thirty-six games in all last term.

Momo Sylla

The stand-in wing-back claimed four goals in his nineteen outings during Season 2002/03. Indeed, the period began rather well for Sylla with the Ivory Coast player (who is very versatile and can play a number of positions) scoring in two of the campaign's first three outings when both Aberdeen (4-0, 10.8.02) and FC Basel (3-1, 14.8.02) were beaten. The occasions of his other two goals were the Scottish Cup tie with St. Mirren (3-0, 25.1.03) and the February league clash with Livingston when he equalised at Celtic Park on the day Henrik Larsson suffered that sickening injury blow of a jaw double fracture.

Neil Lennon

The resolute midfielder started a total of forty six games both home and abroad in Season 2002/03 although he never managed to equal his one goal feat from the 2001/02 period. Irishman Lennon was quite magnificent and simply the best midfielder on the park when Celts recorded an impressive 2-0 victory over Blackburn Rovers at Ewood Park in the November 2002 UEFA Cup tie. After suffering a hamstring injury in Spain during the next round's away leg with Celta Vigo, the player missed seven winter games before returning for the SPL clash with Partick Thistle at Firhill at the beginning of February. From then until the end of the season at Rugby Park, he was an ever-present except when he was rested for the Scottish Cup encounter with First Division St. Johnstone at Celtic Park. In the final statistical analysis of the 2002/03 period, it was confirmed that, except for Barry Ferguson at Rangers, Lennon completed more passes than any other player in the Scottish Premier League. His worth to the team cannot be underestimated.

Alan Thompson

Quite simply, without fear of contradiction, Alan Thompson is the best crosser of a ball in Scottish Football today. This was verified at the end of Season 2002/03 when it was shown that he made more successful crosses (74 in total) than any other SPL player. With 209, he also attempted more crosses than anyone else. The Englishman began thirty-nine games in all last term during which time his name was on a dozen goals. Interestingly enough, six of those twelve strikes were recorded in five of the last seven games of the 2002/03 campaign. The week after his penalty conversion had given Celtic the lead at Ibrox in late April, the midfielder was on the score sheet again when Dunfermline lost at East End Park (4-1, 3.5.03). Seven days on, he netted the winner against Hearts in the east end of Glasgow (1-0, 10.5.03) before claiming a double when Dundee keeper Speroni had to pick the ball out of the net six times during Celtic's final home game of the season (6-2, 14.5.03). Many of those who follow Celtic are probably not aware that when Thompson was just sixteen, he broke his neck in a car accident outside Durham and was told by a specialist that, because of three broken vertebrae, he would not play football again!

16

Shaun Maloney

Although the youngster (Celtic Young Player of the Year for the 2002/03 period) only made the starting line-up ten times last season, he did score five goals. With the powerful Stuttgart as opponents in a UEFA Cup clash at Celtic Park in late February, the tie was evenly balanced at 1-1 before Maloney, deputising for the injured Henrik Larsson, pounced on a Dangelmayr mistake and fired past keeper Hildebrand. Not only had this goal given Celts the lead but it also set them on the road to their 100th European victory. The young man also made the headlines some three months later when his double in the 6-2 SPL destruction of Dundee helped keep the championship race well and truly alive. During the last game of the SPL season at Kilmarnock, he was withdrawn early because of injury with a subsequent scan revealing that two bones in his foot had been broken.

Paul Lambert

Captain of both club and country, midfielder Paul Lambert's final count for Season 2002/03 was forty-one starts and six goals. Right at the beginning of proceedings in August, strike number one was delivered against Aberdeen when his delightful shot was the fourth layer on Celtic's Pittodrie cake that afternoon. However, for sheer class, goal number four of the half-dozen would take some beating. After Stuttgart had taken the lead in February's UEFA Cup game at Celtic Park, Lambert equalised with the most sublime strike to cheer boss Martin O'Neill in his temporary seat in the main stand. As the championship crusade reached its latter stages, a stormy Fir Park, Motherwell in early May was the venue for another two crackers from the skipper. With Celtic leading 2-0 in the heavy rain, he doubled his side's tally courtesy of, firstly, a powerful finish from Shaun Maloney's low cross and then, secondly, a wicked dipping volley that left keeper Woods nowhere to put the Bhoys back on top of the SPL on goal difference.

HEADLINE NEWS...HEADLINE NE

CELTIC MADE THE FOLLOWING FOOTBALL HEADLINES DURING SEASON 2002/03.

WHAT WAS THE OCCASION?   **THE CLUE IS IN THE DATE!**

1. **'THAT'LL DO NICELY, STAN'** Sunday Mirror, **20.4.03**

2. **'HOME AND DRY WITH AWAY GOAL'** Daily Mail, **13.12.02**

3. **'THE SILENCER'** Daily Mail, **28.4.03**

4. **'IT'S BREACH OF THE PREECE'** Daily Record, **4.11.02**

5. **'THAT'S FINAL'** Daily Mail, **25.4.03**

6. **'THEY CAN'T CALL US MICKEY MOUSE NOW'** Daily Mail, **21.3.03**

7. **'CELTIC JUGGERNAUT PICKS UP PACE'** Daily Mail, **10.3.03**

8. **'TEARFUL FINALE FOR THE HEROES'** Daily Mail, **22.5.03**

9. **'ROVER AND OUT'** Daily Mail, **15.11.02**

10. **'AL-MOST THERE'** Sunday Mirror, **11.5.03**

ANSWERS ON PAGE 62

MISSING WORD QUIZ

FILL IN THE NAME OF THE MISSING CELT FROM THIS
SELECTION OF SEASON 2002/03 FOOTBALL HEADLINES.
THE CLUE IS IN THE DATE!

1　'……. PSYCHES OUT CABALLERO' 23.12.02

2　'….. HEADS GREAT ESCAPE CAST' 3.3.03

3　'……. STUNS KOP TO THE CORE' 21.3.03

4　'…… THE RELIEF STRIKER FOR CELTIC' 5.10.02

5　'McLEISH FINALLY FALLS UNDER ……. SPELL' 9.3.03

6　'……. IS QUICK TO FIND HIS FEET ON THE BIG STAGE' 21.2.03

7　'…… POWERS CLINICAL CELTIC' 4.5.03

8　'…….. SPOT ON FOR GLORY' 11.5.03

9　'THOMPSON AND YOUNG ……. HIT VISITORS WITH BOTH
　　BARRELS' 15.5.03

10　'……. DOUBLE ALL IN VAIN AS THE HEAT – AND THE CHEATS –
　　CONSPIRE TO DEFEAT THE BHOYS' 22.5.03

ANSWERS ON PAGE 62

THE QUOTES QUIZ
- WHO SAID THAT

1 'I got an elbow but these things happen. It's two or three stitches but hardly worth mentioning.'

2 'When they scored their third I actually thought they'd gone off to the centre of town to celebrate.'

3 'It was either me or Tom Boyd next and I would have probably hit the corner flag.'

4 'He is as brave as a lion and it will take more than that to keep him out of the match on Thursday.'

5 'There's no other place in Europe like Celtic Park and I will never find anything else like it.'

6 'We out-fought them, out-played them and out-tackled them.'

7 'I had to produce with Henrik out. I don't get too many chances, so I had to grasp it with both hands.'

8 'I was planning a celebration if I scored to mark the birth by rocking my arms like a baby's cradle. But I was so excited I forgot to do it.'

9 'You just have to blank out what's going on behind the goal and what people are saying to you and treat it as you would when you practiced it. I took a long run-up to give the 'keeper something to think about.'

10 'It's up to the individuals who make the comments, but those comments can come back to haunt you and you can be left with egg on your face.'

ANSWERS ON PAGE 62

SEASON 2002/03 CELTIC AND THE SCOTTISH CUP AND CIS CUPS QUIZ

1. What was the common link between the October CIS Cup third-round tie and the March Scottish Cup fifth-round tie?

2. Who netted his first goal of the season in the above CIS Cup game?

3. Name the Celtic scorer, in regulation time, when the team met Partick Thistle in the fourth round of the CIS Cup tournament.

4. What was the penalty-kick shoot-out score that night after extra-time?

5. Who claimed a double when St. Mirren provided the opposition in Round 3 of the Scottish Cup?

6. What two factors united Celtic's opponents in the third and fourth rounds of the Scottish Cup competition?

7. Where was Celtic's next port of call after their Scottish Cup game of Sunday 23 February?

8. Whose goal was wrongly judged to be offside in the CIS Cup final with Rangers?

9. What injury did Chris Sutton sustain during the above game?

10. Only three of the previous Thursday's Anfield heroes began the Inverness CT Scottish Cup tie in late March. Name them.

ANSWERS ON PAGE 62

SEASON 2002/03

OLD FIRM QUIZ

1. What was the score in the first Old Firm game of the season?

2. Name the player who gave Celtic the lead that day.

3. What was unusual about the 'Bhoys' first goal in the early December Ibrox clash?

4. With the score balanced at 1-1 in the above game, whose effort hit the post and then ran along the goal line without actually crossing it?

5. Henrik Larsson netted the winner when the teams met again at Celtic Park in March. True or false?

6. Who scored for Celtic in the CIS Insurance Cup final at Hampden?

7. Celtic's penalty that day was awarded after Amoruso fouled which player in the box?

8. In the last Old Firm clash of the season, both Johan Mjallby and Stilian Petrov failed to make the starting line-up. True or false?

9. Who led the team out as captain that Sunday lunchtime?

10. Name the scorers for Celtic on this memorable day.

ANSWERS ON PAGE 63

CELTIC IN EUROPE QUIZ

SEASON 2002/03

1. Who were Celtic's first European opponents last season?
2. Name the scorer of the dramatic late, late goal which ensured a 3-1 victory that August night.
3. What was the aggregate score when Celtic met Suduva of Lithuania in the UEFA Cup?
4. After netting the winner against Blackburn Rovers at Celtic Park, Henrik Larsson's Euro tally now stood at goals. Fill in the missing number.
5. What was rather special about this new total?
6. Whose stunning header against Blackburn Rovers at Ewood Park finally ended the English side's slim hope of UEFA Cup progress?
7. What was a first in the club's history when Celta Vigo were despatched from last season's UEFA Cup competition?
8. Name all three Celtic scorers when Stuttgart were beaten 3-1 in Glasgow.
9. Prior to the Liverpool/Celtic game, John Hartson had been on the winning side at Anfield on two previous occasions with Arsenal. True or false?
10. Who was the first-half replacement for the injured Paul Lambert in the away leg of the semi-final with Boavista?

ANSWERS ON PAGE 63

CELTIC AND THE SPL QUIZ

SEASON 2002/03

1. Who scored Celtic's first and last goals of the SPL season?

2. Prior to Christmas last season, the Bhoys netted five times (on two separate occasions) and seven times in the league. Name the SPL opponents.

3. Can you name the only player who started every SPL game up until the Dens Park encounter of early April?

4. Who was top scorer in the league against Rangers in Season 2002/03?

5. How many times did Celtic score four goals away from home?

6. Can you name their SPL opponents on these occasions?

7. In early May, Paul Lambert's two goals against Motherwell were the midfielder's first league strikes of the campaign. True or false?

8. Apart from Henrik Larsson, who was the only other Celt to net twice in consecutive SPL games?

9. Who claimed the winner against Hearts at Celtic Park in the penultimate home game of the campaign?

10. Two players netted twice in the final home game of Season 2002/03. Can you name them?

ANSWERS ON PAGE 63

ACROSS THE BORDER

Victories over both Blackburn Rovers (at Ewood Park) and Liverpool at (Anfield) during the glorious UEFA Cup campaign of Season 2002/03 meant that Martin O'Neill's undefeated record in England stretched to eleven games. Here's a reminder of that excellent unbeaten sequence of results, up to and including last season:

22.1.01 - **NORWICH 2 CELTIC 4**
(Moravcik (2), Larsson, Burchill)

14.7.01 – **QPR 0 CELTIC 2**
(Larsson, Moravcik)

1.8.01 – **MANCHESTER UNITED 3 CELTIC 4**
(Sutton, Lennon, Lambert, Moravcik)

9.4.02 – **LEICESTER 0 CELTIC 1**
(Hartson)

7.5.02– **LEEDS 1 CELTIC 4**
(Thompson, Larsson, Hartson, Maloney)

13.5.02 – **ARSENAL 1 CELTIC 1**
(Thompson)

10.7.02– **PORTSMOUTH 2 CELTIC 3**
(Sylla, Petta, Healy)

13.7.02 – **QPR 3 CELTIC 7**
(Fernandez (2), Healy, Sutton, Hartson, Maloney, Sylla)

7.8.02 – **TOTTENHAM 1 CELTIC 1**
(Maloney)

14.11.02 – **BLACKBURN ROVERS 0 CELTIC 2**
(Larsson, Sutton)

20.3.03 – **LIVERPOOL 0 CELTIC 2**
(Thompson, Hartson)

TO SAY THE LEAST, A RATHER IMPRESSIVE RECORD!

The big man

Some players truly excel in the white heat of an Old Firm clash whilst others, quite frankly, find the occasion beyond them and cannot handle the very real mental and physical pressure often associated with this famous fixture. There can be no doubt that Celtic's lionhearted John Hartson, a big man in the real sense of the word, falls into the former category when it comes to games with Rangers.

In the vital final two Celtic/Rangers SPL games of last season when the title race was still up for grabs, it was the big Welshman who netted the winning strike on both occasions. At Celtic Park in early March, with some fifty-eight minutes on the clock and the score still 0-0, a deep penetrating Alan Thompson ball was won in the air by Chris Sutton (despite the close attention of Amoruso and Bonnissel, two defenders in blue) for the unmarked Hartson to volley powerfully past the German Klos in goal. Several weeks later in the Govan district of Glasgow, the striker claimed Celtic's second of the day (in the 2-1 victory) from close range following good work by both Didier Agathe and Henrik Larsson. It should not be forgotten he also 'won' the penalty that Alan Thompson converted to give the Bhoys an early lead that Sunday lunchtime.

John Hartson arrived in Glasgow in August 2001 after manager Martin O'Neill had agreed a £6.5 million fee with Coventry for his services. His first goals in the green of Celtic followed two months later when John claimed a hat-trick in the 5-1 crushing of Dundee United. By the end of that season, the hit-man had netted 24 times in 35 games with a memorable double being recorded in the April tussle with Livingston at Celtic Park (5-1, 6.4.02) when the Championship was secured for the second time in just two years.

Last season, there were many memorable occasions in addition to the two aforementioned Old Firm encounters. Back in mid-September, Hartson scored the only goal of the game when visitors Hibernian returned to the capital empty handed and then, in early November, warmed the home support with four hot ones as Celtic devastated Aberdeen with seven of the best in the season's only 7-0 SPL thrashing. Hearts were then treated to a Hartson hat-trick on Boxing Day (4-2, 26.12.02) and, the week before that Old Firm Celtic Park winner in March, his Glasgow double against Hibernian (3-2, 2.3.03) meant that all three points were in the bag after another extremely hard-fought league encounter.

Also that month, Celtic secured a famous 2-0 away win in the UEFA Cup tie with Liverpool. Perhaps not surprisingly, the player's tremendous Anfield strike that Thursday night (a vicious shot from outside the box that absolutely flew past Dudek in goal) was voted Goal of the Season in the Celtic Player of the Year awards for 2002/03. In the eyes of many supporters, however, Hartson's winning goals in the two aforementioned SPL Old Firm clashes sit side by side with that rather special Anfield strike - for obvious reasons! The stuff of dreams, indeed.

John Hartson - a real big man and a real big striker. Respect!

John Hartson

King of Goals

It is a rare breed of player that can return to first-team action a matter of weeks after having suffered an appalling injury. Who would have thought that Henrik Larsson, a mere five weeks after shattering his jaw in an accidental collision with Livingston's Gus Bahoken, would be ready to face the UEFA Cup might of Liverpool in mid-March? Certainly not those fans at Celtic Park, that early February day, who had witnessed the heroic legend being carried from the field with a double-fracture of his jaw! Amazingly, the striker had recovered in time for the visit of Liverpool and, true to form, netted his side's only goal of the game right at the start of that crucial first-leg European tie.

At the end of Season 2001/02, Larsson sat proudly at the top of the scoring chart with a final tally of thirty-five goals from forty-seven games. It is worth noting that, in both domestic and European outings that year, he claimed the deciding strike in ten separate encounters. Last season was even better and he finished the campaign streets ahead of his closest rivals with forty-four goals - an astonishing average of nearly a goal a game! Larsson also had more shots on target (67) than any other SPL striker.

In the very first game of last season, Henrik's two goals ensured a 2-1 victory over Dunfermline and, the following month, it was a case of hat-tricks in the UEFA Cup tie with FK Suduva (8-1, 19.9.02) and the SPL clash with Kilmarnock (5-0, 28.9.02) as Celtic fired on all fronts. With double strikes in consecutive league games against, firstly, Rangers at home (3-3, 6.10.02) and, secondly, Hearts at Gorgie Road, Edinburgh (4-1, 20.10.02), the player was already nearing the twenty goal mark before the end of October. Outwith the domestic scene, the mercurial Swede's winning goal (and only goal of the game) in the UEFA Cup, first-leg encounter with Blackburn Rovers meant that he had become the most prolific scorer for a Scottish club in Europe. Ally McCoist's long-standing record of 21 in all European competitions had now been surpassed.

After scoring against Blackburn Rovers for the second time (at Ewood Park in the return leg), the goals continued to flow and Larsson netted in another four consecutive matches when Partick Thistle, Livingston, Celta Vigo and Motherwell provided the opposition. December/January's tally was just as impressive with his name on the score sheet in six consecutive games – Dundee (2-0, 21.12.02), Hearts (4-2, 26.12.02), Dunfermline (1-0, 29.12.02), Aberdeen (1-1, 2.1.03), St. Mirren (3-0, 25.1.03) and Dundee United (2-0, 29.1.03). Hardly surprisingly, in the final Celtic Park game of last season, it was Henrik Larsson who started the ball rolling when visitors Dundee were crushed 6-2. He was now only one away from an astonishing double century of goals! Both that total (and his 201st goal) duly arrived in the baking heat of Seville when his two superb, second-half headers (and Man of the Match display in the UEFA Cup final against Porto) took the Bhoys so close to another famous European victory.

Voted 'Greatest Ever Foreign Player' in a poll at the club last season, he now stands shoulder to shoulder with the legendary immortals of Celtic Park. There can be no greater compliment.

Henrik Larsson

Lionheart

In truth, many Celtic fans were left quite speechless when Stilian Petrov ran out with the rest of the team prior to the start of the Glasgow UEFA Cup game with Celta Vigo in late November. Their astonishment was entirely understandable considering the fact that, only four days earlier, the Bulgarian midfielder had suffered a horrific mouth wound in a clash with defender Marvin Andrews when Livingston were SPL opponents at the City Stadium. Horrific indeed as the injury required several stitches outside his mouth in addition to some nine or ten inside! 'He is as brave as a lion and it will take more than that to keep him out of the match on Thursday' said Martin O'Neill after the game, perfectly summing up both the player's courage and commitment to Celtic.

Voted Scotland's Young Player of the Year by his fellow professionals for Season 2000/01, Petrov became the first overseas footballer to win this prestigious award, following in the footsteps of other Celtic greats such as Charlie Nicholas and Paul McStay. The powerhouse midfielder made thirty-three starts for the 'Hoops' that season before breaking his ankle in the McDiarmid Park game with St. Johnstone in the middle of March. The following campaign, he famously opened the scoring against Rangers at Ibrox in consecutive Govan encounters – in late September 2001, his wicked free-kick completely deceived Stefan Klos in goal and, in early March 2002 at a windy Ibrox, he slid the ball under the advancing German following a delightful pass from Henrik Larsson.

Last season, Petrov was as inspirational as ever in the middle of the park for his beloved Celtic. Although he claimed his first goal of the SPL season in the August 5-0 destruction of Dundee United and his first double in the 4-0 triumph over Partick Thistle (both home games), his most important strike in the first-half of the campaign was at Easter Road in early December. With both Larsson and Sutton missing through injury, the Bhoys returned home later that Wednesday night having secured all three championship points after a hard-fought 1-0 victory in the capital. The goal came courtesy of a certain young Bulgarian!

On the European stage in February, the player's superb shot from an extremely tight angle, midway through the second period, gave Celtic a vital 3-1 advantage to take to Stuttgart in the UEFA Cup. Speaking of the German outfit, Petrov was due to succeed their midfielder Krassimir Balakov as captain of his country at the end of last season. It is worth remembering the words of Kevin Keegan who was England manager at the time his side drew 1-1 with Bulgaria in Sofia in 1999. After this international game, he said that Petrov 'against England, displayed skills, intellect and maturity, not only beyond his years but also well beyond the capabilities of the vast majority of his more experienced colleagues on the field.'

In May 2003, as the domestic league campaign headed towards an exciting close conclusion, Stilian netted a double in consecutive away encounters with Dunfermline (4-1, 3.5.03) and Motherwell (4-0, 7.5.03) as Celtic closed in on Rangers. Indeed, it was Petrov's name on the crucial opening goal in both of the aforementioned SPL clashes.

No wonder so many are of the opinion that STAN'S THE MAN!

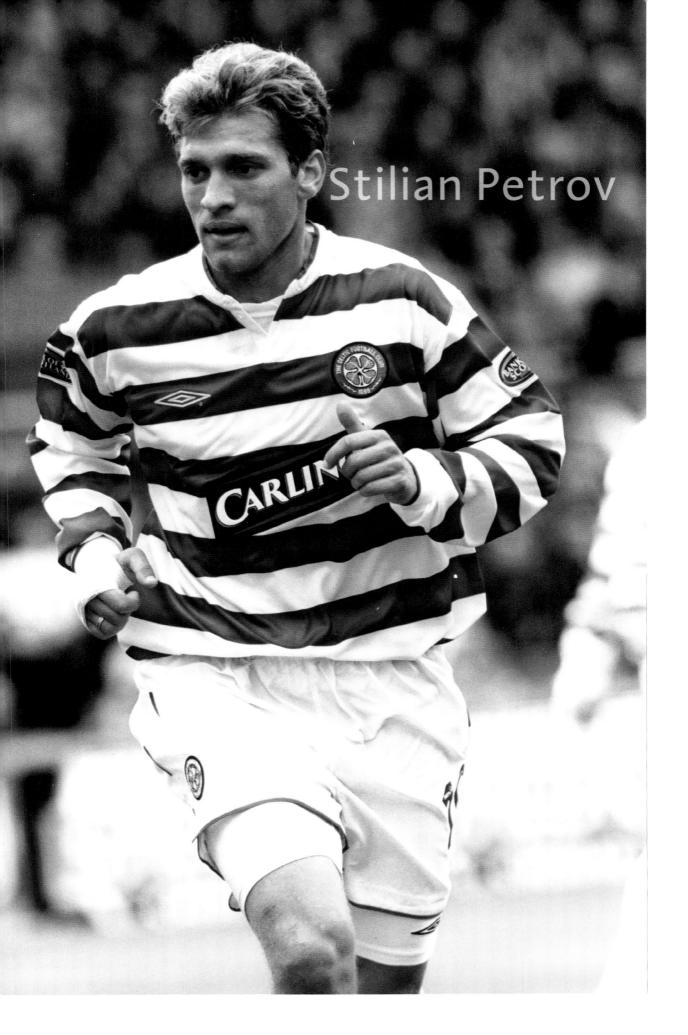

Stilian Petrov

Player of the Year

SEASON 2002/03

Even the most biased of football supporters in Scotland would surely agree that this giant of a man has developed tremendously as a player since arriving in the country and making his Celtic debut (in the 3-1 Glasgow victory over Dunfermline) back in September 2001. Being virtually unbeatable in the air (regardless of the calibre of opposition) and a veritable tower of strength on the ground, Balde has won the hearts and minds of all who follow the team. Certainly it came as little surprise to the Celtic masses when he was named Player of the Year in the club's inaugural award ceremony last season when an astonishing 40,000 fans voted.

The unyielding defender was just one of three Celts (Belgian Joos Valgaeren and Swede Henrik Larsson were the others) who started over a half century of games for the club in the 2002/03 period and was the only rearguard member to claim a double last season. The match in question was the 3-0 CIS Insurance Cup semi-final clash with Dundee United at Hampden in early February. Indeed, Balde actually totalled four goals last term, the other two coming in the SPL home encounters with Livingston (2-0, 1.9.02) and Aberdeen (7-0, 3.11.02). By comparison, in his first year in green, he made thirty-eight starts with two goals in each of the three Scottish domestic competitions. In Europe, apart from the trip to Lithuania for the return-leg of the FK Suduva clash, the defender was an ever-present in Celtic's glorious UEFA campaign with his tournament performances receiving rave reviews both home and abroad. It must be said also that Balde was most unfortunate to be booked twice in the Seville final with Porto.

On the night of the aforementioned award ceremony and his Player of the Year accolade, Martin O'Neill said 'I was absolutely delighted for him because he has been terrific for us throughout this season. He has almost improved game by game and especially in Europe some of his performances have been exceptional. I am pleased for him because he has worked hard and his improvement has been there for all to see.'

Nothing more really needs to be said.

Bobo Balde

Simply Sutton
- The Best

It looked as if Chris Sutton's season had come to a premature end when the striker snapped his left wrist (following a penalty-box collision with Bobo Balde) and was carried from the field in agony during the CIS Insurance Cup final with Rangers at Hampden in mid-March. Just weeks later however (and, understandably, not fully-fit), he appeared as a first-half substitute in place of the injured Paul Lambert in the UEFA semi-final against Boavista in Portugal. It came as little surprise when, late in the game, he was involved in the move that led to Larsson's historic goal and confirmed Celtic's place in the Seville final.

Having successfully filled both centre-half and centre-forward positions with Norwich earlier in his career, Sutton went on to form the feared SAS partnership with Alan Shearer at Blackburn Rovers and he led the English Premiership scoring charts with eighteen goals in one season during his time at Ewood Park. Chelsea manager Gianluca Vialli then paid some £10 million to take the player south to London before Martin O'Neill made Chris his first Celtic signing. At that time, the fee of £6 million was a Scottish transfer record. Early on in his initial season at the club, Sutton famously scored in both the first and last minutes of a rather memorable 6-2 rout as title holders Rangers were swept aside at Celtic Park on a late August afternoon. His partnership with Henrik Larsson paid royal dividends throughout that treble campaign and watching the two of them in tandem was one of the year's true delights for all 'Hoop' lovers. Although injury called to play a major part throughout the following year (Period 2001/02), he still totalled twenty-nine games and seven goals for the club.

Last season, he netted in three of the opening four encounters when Aberdeen (4-0, 10.8.02), FC Basel (3-1, 14.8.02) and Dundee United (5-0, 17.8.02) provided both domestic and foreign opposition before claiming a double when Kilmarnock were thrashed 5-0 in late September. On some occasions, manager Martin O'Neill positioned him to great effect just behind strikers Larsson and Hartson. Indeed, filling such a role in the UEFA Cup 'Battle of Britain' clash with his old side Blackburn Rovers at Ewood Park in November, Sutton was absolutely immense, nullifying and outplaying their Turkish playmaker (and ex-Ranger) Tugay in the process. An additional pleasure for the thousands of visitors was, of course, his awesome goal - a bullet header from Petrov's corner that sealed another celebrated victory on English soil and sent the Celtic masses into ecstasy. At the end of the game, Blackburn manager Graeme Souness suggested that Chris Sutton was the best player on the pitch.

Celtic's massive travelling support that night would surely have echoed those sentiments wholeheartedly.

Chris Sutton

Pick of the Trophy Rooms
BOVISTA CARAVEL 1975

With the 2002/03 UEFA Cup semi-final 2-1 aggregate win over Boavista of Portugal still fresh in the mind, here is a reminder of the previous occasion that the sides met in European competition. After being drawn together in the European Cup Winners' Cup of Season 1975/76, Celts travelled to Portugal for the first leg. Despite creating many chances, the home side were kept at bay by goalkeeper Peter Latchford whose wonderful display that evening included a penalty save near the end of the regulation ninety minutes. Somewhat unlucky, Boavista had to settle for a 0-0 draw.

Two weeks later, the Celtic Park return started quite sensationally when Kenny Dalglish scored in the first minute of the tie, helping to calm any early nerves on the night. Subsequent goals from Edvaldsson and 'Dixie' Deans in each half saw Celtic through to the quarter-final stage of the competition after a 3-1 victory.

22.10.75 BOAVISTA 0 CELTIC 0

Celtic: Latchford, McGrain, Lynch, P.McCluskey, MacDonald, Edvaldsson, Callaghan, McNamara, Wilson, Hood and Lennox.

5.11.75   CELTIC 3 BOAVISTA 1

Celtic: Latchford, McGrain, Lynch, P.McCluskey, MacDonald, Edvaldsson, G.McCluskey, Dalglish, Deans, McNamara and Callaghan.

Pick of the Trophy Rooms

SAMOTHRACE STATUETTE 1970

Without a doubt, Season 1966/67 was the most marvellous in Celtic's long and illustrious history. Three years later, however, the club stood on the brink of greatness once more when both European and domestic glory beckoned yet again. At home, the League Championship was secured for a fifth successive season with second-place Rangers twelve points adrift at the final countdown. Although beaten in the final of the Scottish Cup, both the League Cup (also a fifth successive triumph) and the Glasgow Cup made their way to the trophy room.

After disposing of the 'unbeatable' English Champions Leeds United at the two-leg semi-final stage of the European Cup (with a 1-0 Elland Road result and a 2-1 Hampden triumph), Celtic made the final for the second time in just four years. However, it was the Dutch of Feyenoord who lifted the trophy after a 2-1 extra-time victory. As they say, so close yet so far.

Presented by the world renowned French sports newspaper 'France Football', this trophy (a replica of the famed work of art that resides in the L'Ouvre Museum, Paris) confirms Celtic as 'European Team of the Year' for Season 1969/70 and is, indeed, the most prestigious of honours.

FRANCE-FOOTBALL ADIDAS
CHALLENGE EUROPEEN DE FOOTBALL 1970
CELTIC - LASGOW

If You Know The History

CHARLES PATRICK TULLY

A true Celtic legend, Charlie Tully arrived from Belfast in 1948 following his £8000 transfer. In truth, the 'Hoops' (whose last championship was in 1938) were in dire need of a hero at that time having only just avoided relegation. Charlie would soon become the fans' darling!

In 1951, after lifting the Scottish Cup for the first time since the late 1930s, Celtic then claimed one of their most famous trophies – the St. Mungo Cup. Aberdeen were beaten 3-2 in the final of this competition (part of the Festival of Great Britain celebrations) with one of Tully's mazy dribbles being the prelude to Walsh's winner on the great day. Although Charlie missed the final of the Coronation Cup in May 1953 through injury, he had set-up Bertie Peacock's for the deciding goal when Manchester United fell 2-1 at the semi-final stage. This magnificent trophy now also resides at Celtic Park following the final victory over Hibernian.

A League and Scottish Cup double (the club's first in some forty years!) followed in 1953/54 with League Cup success in both the 1956/57 and 1957/58 seasons. Not surprisingly, when Rangers were crushed 7-1 in the League Cup final of October 1957, Tully turned in a five star performance. Or should that be a seven star performance? Probably the most famous Charlie Tully story centred round a Scottish Cup tie with Falkirk at Brockville in 1953 when he scored direct from a corner. Not entirely satisfied, the referee asked for the kick to be retaken and watched in amazement as 'Cheeky' scored again! Celtic, having been 2-0 down, went on to win the game 3-2. Amazingly, the player had previously performed this exact feat in a Northern Ireland/England international encounter.

NA
LEAGUE CHAMPI
SCOTTISH CUP
SCOTTISH LEAGU
CORONATION CU
ST. MUNGO'S CU

CHARLES PATRICK TULLY
1924 - 1971

INTERNATIONAL HONOURS

NORTHERN IRELAND

VERSUS ENGLAND
1948
1949
1952
1955
VERSUS SCOTLAND
1951
1952
1953
VERSUS WALES
1953
VERSUS FRANCE
1952
VERSUS SPAIN
1958

Chasing Rainbows

MEMORIES OF A JOYOUS UEFA JOURNEY

CELTIC 8 FK SUDUVA 1

Celtic's UEFA Cup campaign of last season began back in September 2002 when the Lithuanian minnows of FK Suduva were swept aside 8-1 at Celtic Park. Goals from Lennon, Larsson (3), Petrov, Sutton, Lambert and substitute John Hartson did the damage. On the eve of his birthday (there would be thirty-one candles on tomorrow's cake), Henrik Larsson's three goals that night meant the Swede had equalled Ally McCoist's record of twenty-one European goals. After the game, manager Martin O'Neill commented that he would not have substituted the player if he had realised the record was up for grabs! Still, it was hoped, there would be plenty other nights to come.

Celtic: Douglas, Valgaeren, Balde, Laursen (Crainey), Sylla, Lambert, Lennon (Fernandez), Petrov, Guppy, Sutton and Larsson (Hartson).

FK SUDUVA 0 CELTIC 2

Following the tremendous scoring exploits of the first-leg when the Bhoys were only one short of their best-ever score in Europe (the Finns of Kokkola were thrashed 9-0 in Glasgow back in 1970), the return fixture in Lithuania was, naturally, no more than a formality. Goals from Fernandez (his first for the club since arriving from Livingston) and Thompson gave Celts victory in a game which was watched by some 1000 spectators. Young John Kennedy made his European debut in defence - John Hartson missed a penalty!

Celtic: Gould, McNamara (Miller), Crainey, Kennedy (Smith), Agathe, Thompson, Maloney, Healy, Petta (Lynch), Fernandez and Hartson.

CELTIC 1 BLACKBURN ROVERS 0

The English Premiership outfit managed by Graeme Souness (player/manager of Rangers in another life) came, saw but certainly did not conquer! On a night when goalkeeper Rab Douglas would just not be beaten, it was the arrival of substitute John Hartson that helped turn the game for Celtic. His blocked effort, following an Alan Thompson corner with just five minutes left on the clock, was steered home by Henrik Larsson thus ensuring plenty of Hallowe'en celebrations in the east end of Glasgow.

Celtic: Douglas, Valgaeren, Balde, Laursen, Agathe (Sylla), Lennon, Lambert (Hartson), Petrov, Thompson, Sutton and Larsson.

BLACKBURN ROVERS 0 CELTIC 2

Some 8000 travelling Celtic fans watched a truly magnificent display of football as their team, courtesy of goals from both Larsson (a delightful chip over American World Cup keeper Brad Friedel) and Sutton (a powerfully sublime second-half header that flashed into the net) progressed to the next round of the competition on the back of a 3-0 aggregate score. In truth, the Bhoys were just too strong for their worthy Premiership opponents.

Celtic: Douglas, Valgaeren, Balde, Laursen, Agathe (Sylla), Lennon, Petrov (Thompson), Sutton, Guppy, Hartson (Lambert) and Larsson.

CELTIC 1 CELTA VIGO 0

An early second-half headed goal by the King (his 24th in Europe) was the only difference between the sides when the impressive Spaniards of Celta Vigo (sitting third in Primera Liga, one of the strongest European leagues) lost on Scottish soil in late November. In addition, Celtic were halfway to rewriting a section of their history books as, in some forty years of competition, the Hoops had never disposed of a Spanish club.

Celtic: Douglas, Valgaeren, Balde, Laursen, Agathe (Sylla), Lennon, Petrov, Guppy (Thompson), Sutton, Hartson and Larson.

CELTA VIGO 2 CELTIC 1

Celts lost in a rather tense Balaidos Stadium but nevertheless made it to the last sixteen with John Hartson's drilled shot (from a Sutton knock down) just enough to take them through on away goals. Historically, it was the first time since the heady days of 1980 that the club had remained in Europe beyond the Christmas period.

Celtic: Douglas, Valgaeren, Balde, Laursen, Agathe, Lennon (Lambert), Petrov, Sutton, Thompson, Hartson (McNamara) and Larsson.

CELTIC 3 STUTTGART 1

With both Larsson and Hartson missing from the starting line-up of this fourth round tie (the Swede had sustained a double fracture of his jaw in the Livingston SPL clash some days earlier and the Welshman was suspended), it was the German outfit who took the lead despite being down to ten men after defender Bordon had been dismissed early on. However, subsequent goals from Paul Lambert, Shaun Maloney and (new daddy) Stilian Petrov meant that Celtic would take a 3-1 advantage to the Gottlieb-Daimler Stadium.

Celtic: Douglas, Valgaeren, Balde (Laursen), McNamara, Agathe, Lambert, Lennon, Petrov, Thompson (Smith), Sutton and Maloney.

STUTTGART 3 CELTIC 2

Although Larsson was still absent, 10,000 green and white cadets celebrated early strikes from both Alan Thompson and Chris Sutton, giving the team an immediate 5-1 aggregate advantage. This left the Germans with too much of a mountain to climb and, even although they subsequently netted three times to win the actual game, Stuttgart became just another famous scalp on Celtic's belt. Incidentally, the evening's goals were the first to be recorded by the club on German soil. In due course, Stuttgart would end Season 2002/03 as runners-up in the highly rated Bundesliga. With thoughts again turning to English Premiership opponents, the Reds of Gerard Houllier's Liverpool were waiting in the (quarter-final) wings and, as Rab Douglas had jokingly suggested, Battle of Britain Part 42!

Celtic: Douglas, Valgaeren, Balde, Laursen, Agathe, Lambert (Maloney), Thompson, Lennon, Petrov, Sutton (McNamara) and Hartson.

CELTIC 1 LIVERPOOL 1

Despite being sidelined for all of five weeks, it took Henrik Larsson less than three minutes to raise the roof at Celtic Park with the opening goal. Then, with the game still in its early stages, England striker Heskeymade levelled matters to make it 1-1. With no more scoring that night and advantage to Liverpool, the stage was set for a titanic Anfield showdown. Several English press reports after the game seemed to suggest that Celtic's chance of progression in the tournament had already come and gone and Liverpool, following their home, second-leg in one week's time, would be filling one of the 2002/03 UEFA Cup semi-final places. Oh dear!

Celtic: Douglas, Mjallby, Balde, Valgaeren, Smith, Lennon, Petrov, Sutton, Thompson (Guppy), Hartson and Larsson (Lambert).

LIVERPOOL 0 CELTIC 2

Regardless of the fact that both Didier Agathe and Chris Sutton were missing through injury, Celtic proved too strong for their illustrious hosts and netted in each half of the match. The famous Kop was silenced! Alan Thompson claimed the first goal with a low, powerful free-kick just before the break and then, late in the second period, Welsh international John Hartson's amazing strike (Goal of the Season in the Celtic Player of the Year awards) soared past Dudek to thicken the icing on the evening's rather sweet cake. For the many thousands of fans who had travelled to Merseyside for the game, it was certainly a night to remember.

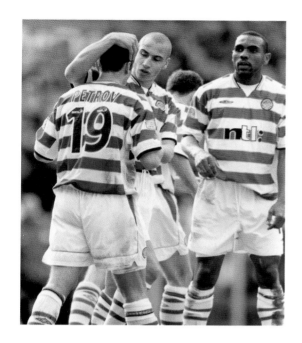 

CELTIC 1 BOAVISTA 1

Early in the second-half of this encounter with Boavista of Portugal, Super Swede hit his 26th European goal which levelled the game one minute after Joos Valgaeren's unfortunate own-goal. It could have been number twenty-seven for Larsson later on in the tie (with some fifteen minutes left on the clock) but goalkeeper (and captain) Ricardo saved his penalty attempt. As the encounter ended 1-1, it meant that Celts would have to score (at least) in the Do Bessa Stadium return clash in order to reach a European final and emulate those legendary sides back in 1967 and 1970.

Celtic: Douglas, Mjallby, Balde, Valgaeren, Agathe (Sylla), Lambert, Lennon, Petrov, (Fernandez), Thompson, Hartson and Larsson.

BOAVISTA 0 CELTIC 1

With the game in its latter stages and less than fifteen minutes play remaining, Boavista's tiresome tactics of containment were on the verge of paying dividends before that man Larsson claimed his 40th of the season (and the most significant?) to ensure a Spanish showdown with Porto in Seville the following month. It would be the club's first European final in over thirty years. Somehow everyone just knew that super Swede's name would be on any winning goal that glorious night! Incidentally, the champions of Portugal had beaten the Italians of Lazio 4-1 (on aggregate) thus earning the right to a UEFA Cup final slot. It is surely worth recalling that, as well as Lazio, high calibre teams such as Paris Saint-Germain, Bordeaux, Sporting Lisbon and Chelsea had all fallen on route to the final.

Celtic: Douglas, Mjallby, Balde, Valgaeren (Smith), Agathe, Lennon, Petrov, Lambert (Sutton), Thompson, Hartson and Larsson.

CELTIC 2 PORTO 3

In truth Seville (or for that matter any other major European city where football is played) had never seen anything like it - an astonishing 75,000 plus Celtic fans arrived in the beautiful Spanish city for the UEFA Cup Final of Season 2002/03! Whatever the eventual win or lose outcome, these wonderful fans were going to enjoy the occasion. Played in the searing heat and humidity of Estadio Olimpico, the game itself was evenly balanced before Derlei gave Porto the lead on the stroke of half-time. However, just two minutes into the second period, Celtic drew level when Henrik Larsson's superbly judged header (from Agathe's deep cross) went in off the post and became his 200th goal for the club. Russian international Alenichev then restored Porto's advantage before Man of the Match Larsson (with another headed goal but this time from Thompson's corner) squared the game for the second time. In extra-time, with the Bhoys down to ten men after Bobo Balde had been dismissed, Derlei netted his second of the night when a penalty shoot-out seemed to be on the cards. Cruel as it was, sad as it was, the dream had finally come to an end.

Although the UEFA Cup would not be returning with the team to Glasgow, the Celtic masses all agreed that Martin O'Neill's players had done them proud. It had been the most amazing journey for these exceptional supporters who, needless to say, will always walk on with hope in their hearts.

Celtic: Douglas, Mjallby, Balde, Valgaeren (Laursen), Agathe, Lennon, Lambert (McNamara), Petrov (Maloney), Thompson, Sutton and Larsson.
Petrov, Thompson (Smith), Sutton and Maloney.

ALMOST PERFECT

Throughout Season 2002/03's Scottish Premier League campaign, the Bhoys remained unbeaten at home, dropping only two points out of a possible fifty-seven. During this remarkable run of Celtic Park games, they scored fifty-six goals with the loss of only twelve. How many of the following matches do you remember?

3.8.02 **Celtic 2 Dunfermline 1**
Larsson (2)

17.8.02 **Celtic 5 Dundee United 0**
Larsson, Sutton, Petrov, McNamara, Hartson

1.9.02 **Celtic 2 Livingston 0**
Larsson, Balde

14.9.02 **Celtic 1 Hibernian 0**
Hartson

28.9.02 **Celtic 5 Kilmarnock 0**
Larsson (3), Sutton (2)

6.10.02 **Celtic 3 Rangers 3**
Larsson (2), Sutton

3.11.02 **Celtic 7 Aberdeen 0**
Hartson (4), Larsson, Balde, Maloney

17.11.02 **Celtic 4 Partick Thistle 0**
Petrov (2), Larsson, Whyte og

1.12.02 **Celtic 3 Motherwell 1**
Larsson, Valgaeren, Leitch og

21.12.02 **Celtic 2 Dundee 0**
Larsson, Hartson

26.12.02 **Celtic 4 Hearts 2**
Hartson (3), Larsson

29.12.02 **Celtic 1 Dunfermline 0**
Larsson

29.1.03 **Celtic 2 Dundee United 0**
Larsson, Hartson

9.2.03 **Celtic 2 Livingston 1**
Sutton, Sylla

2.3.03 **Celtic 3 Hibernian 2**
Hartson (2), Mjallby

8.3.03 **Celtic 1 Rangers 0**
Hartson

13.4.03 **Celtic 2 Kilmarnock 0**
Larsson, Petrov

10.5.03 **Celtic 1 Hearts 0**
Thompson

14.5.03 **Celtic 6 Dundee 2**
Thompson (2), Maloney (2), Larsson, Mjallby

AGAINST ALL ODDS

SCOTTISH PREMIER LEAGUE 27 APRIL 2003

RANGERS 1 CELTIC 2
Thompson (28) Hartson (42)

Less than three days after contesting a hard, strength-sapping UEFA Cup semi-final in Portugal, second-place Celtic travelled to meet league-leaders Rangers in what many neutrals assumed to be (virtually) a title-clinching win for the Govan outfit. A home victory, they suggested, was surely a foregone conclusion. After all, the Light Blues had not dropped a single point at Ibrox in the championship race and, being eight clear at the top, were under less pressure than their Old Firm rivals. In addition, it was argued, not having been subjected to the rigours of a European game (or, for that matter, modern European travel!), they would be far fresher come kick-off. But, by early afternoon and the final whistle that Sunday, it was apparent that Celtic had not read the script!

Although both Caniggia and de Boer missed early chances for the hosts, Jackie McNamara (captain for the day) nearly scored a freakish goal when his long ball into the box was missed by attackers and defenders alike and bounced off the post to safety with Klos beaten. Continuing to push forward, Celtic were awarded a penalty by referee Dallas when Amoruso, with a clumsy challenge, felled big John Hartson in the area. Alan Thompson's conversion was greeted by a kind of hush at one end of the stadium and a kind of celebration at the other! Then, with the visitors in the driving seat, Hartson himself made it two (just before half-time) following a sweeping move by Agathe down the right-hand side. The wing-back's ball inside was cleverly played to the Welshman by Henrik Larsson and he duly obliged, sweeping the ball past Klos. It was the striker's 25th goal of the season and, as it happened, his last of the 2002/03 campaign.

Obviously Rangers would have to go for broke in the second period and, twelve minutes into the half, they confirmed the very fact by pulling one back courtesy of de Boer's header. Despite this revival however, Celtic remained comfortable and ended the game in control with no thoughts yet of handing over the league crown that they had held for the past two seasons. Manager Martin O'Neill's change of formation to a flat back four had been an unqualified success and even the loss of keeper Rab Douglas (in just nine minutes) had not disrupted the team in the slightest.

As the visiting fans enjoyed their Sunday success, they no doubt reflected on the mind-blowing events of the last three days when their team not only qualified for the final of a European competition but also threw the league championship race wide open. At this stage of the season, that was more than enough.

Celtic: Douglas (Broto), Laursen, Valgaeren, Balde, McNamara, Thompson, Lennon, Sutton, Agathe, Hartson (Petrov) and Larsson.

If You Know The History

MANAGERS & WINNERS

WILLIAM MALEY
(1897-1940)
16 League Championships, 14 Scottish
Cups plus Glasgow Exhibition Trophy
(1902) and Empire Exhibition Trophy

JIMMY McSTAY
(1940-1945)
Victory in Europe Cup (1945)

JIMMY McGRORY
(1945-1965)
1 League Championship, 2 Scottish Cups,
2 League Cups plus St. Mungo Cup (1951)
and Coronation Cup (1953)

JOCK STEIN
(1965-1978)
10 League Championships, 8 Scottish Cups,
6 League Cups and the
European Cup (1967)

BILLY McNEILL
(1978-1983)
3 League Championships, 1 Scottish Cup
and 1 League Cup

DAVID HAY
(1983-1987)
1 League Championship and 1 Scottish Cup

BILLY McNEILL
(1987-1991)
1 League Championship and 2 Scottish Cups

TOMMY BURNS
(1994-1997)
1 Scottish Cup

WIM JANSEN
(1997-1998)
1 League Championship and 1 League Cup

KENNY DALGLISH
(Interim Head Coach 2000)
1 League Cup

MARTIN O'NEILL
(2000-)
2 League Championships, 1 Scottish Cup and 1 League Cup

CELTIC TRUE ? CELTIC FALSE ?
CELTIC TRUE ? CELTIC FALSE ?
CELTIC TRUE ? CELTIC FALSE ?
CELTIC TRUE ? CELTIC FALSE ?

1. There is a famous trophy at Celtic Park that bears the inscription 'Won by Rangers FC'. True or false?

2. The temperature was nearly 100 degrees inside the Estadio Olimpico in Portugal for the 2002/03 UEFA Cup final. True or false?

3. Celtic have won the Scottish League Championship a total of 36 times. True or false?

4. Jock Stein's Celtic reached the final of the European Cup (for the second time) back in Season 1970/71. True or false?

5. Kenny Dalglish was the first player to represent Scotland 100 times. True or false?

6. When Pierre Van Hooijdonk scored thirty-two times in Season 1995/96, his closest Premier rival was Ally McCoist with twenty-three goals. True or false?

7. In Season 1978/79, Celtic won the championship by defeating Rangers in their last game of the campaign. True or false?

8. When Martin O'Neill's team secured the domestic treble in Season 2000/01, they had become the first Celtic side to achieve this feat in thirty years. True or false?

9. After the league title success of 1997/98, striker Harald Brattbakk had won five consecutive championship medals. True or false?

10. Lisbon Lion and legendary goalkeeper Ronnie Simpson was 34 before he made his Celtic debut. True or false?

ANSWERS ON PAGE 63

JUST SAY **NO** TO TEN IN A ROW

SCOTTISH PREMIER LEAGUE 2 JANUARY 1998

CELTIC 2 RANGERS 0
Burley (66)
Lambert (87)

By the end of the 1996/97 campaign, Rangers had equalled Celtic's impressive feat of nine consecutive league championships and, prior to this January 1998 clash the following season, they were four points clear at the top of the table with 'TEN-IN-A-ROW' uppermost in their thoughts. The pressure was obviously all on Celtic who, remarkably, had not won this Ne'erday Old firm encounter since 1988, ten years previously.

Early on, Celtic began to take control and, indeed, grow in stature as the game progressed. Although there was no scoring in the first-half, Rangers were fortunate to reach the interval still on level terms such was Celtic's dominance for most of that initial period. However, following a Jackie McNamara neat reverse pass just after the break, Craig Burley opened the scoring when he shot past Andy Goram in goal. After that, it was all one-way traffic with the midfield trio of Burley, Paul Lambert and Morten Wieghorst dominating in that area. Crucially, Marc Rieper and Enrico Annoni neutralised the very real dangers of scoring sensation Marco Negri (three goals in the previous two games, thirty that season so far) and the gifted Brian Laudrup respectively.

Although Norwegian striker Harald Brattbakk had chances to increase the tally, it was midfielder Lambert, just three minutes before the end, who sent the home crowd delirious when his astonishing strike from far out swerved into the top corner with Goram left clawing at air. Victory had been assured with this classic goal - there was certainly no way back for the defending champions. With Rangers lead at the top of the table now cut to just one point, Celtic had passed the test. Perhaps it was an omen but the last time the Hoops won this January fixture, they went on to lift the championship in the same season. Just maybe, the ten-in-a-row blue tide was finally turning.

The rest, as they say, is history.

OLD BHOY

DAVY PROVAN

Extremely well known these days for both his radio and television work, Davie Provan (in his playing days) was brought to Celtic Park by Billy McNeill after 'Caesar' had taken over as manager from the legendary Jock Stein prior to Season 1978/79. This expensive acquisition (at that time, the £120,000 fee paid to Kilmarnock for his services was a record between Scottish clubs) would prove to be a marvellous investment as the player had ability in abundance with the essential skills of both winger and striker. In many ways, he was quite unique and, needless to say, the fans took him to their hearts.

Despite a bad start to the 1978/79 campaign, Celtic bounced back and were genuine title contenders late on in the season. By that time, the scenario was such that if they could defeat defending champions Rangers at Celtic Park in May, the league title was all theirs. Our man duly played his part in that most famous of games which Celtic won 4-2 after being behind (1-0) at half-time. In 1980, at the end of the following season, Davie Provan's name was on the Players' Player of the Year award. During his years at the club, four League Championships, two Scottish Cups and one League Cup graced the trophy rooms. He scored 41 goals in 281 Celtic appearances before his career was tragically cut short by a lingering viral illness. English outfit Nottingham Forest provided the opposition for his testimonial game in November 1987.

Looking back on his Celtic career, a spectacular free kick in the Centenary Scottish Cup final of 1985 brings back the warmest of memories. With less than fifteen minutes on the Hampden clock, Dundee United were 1-0 in front and heading for cup glory before Provan's astonishingly powerful and accurate strike levelled the game. Celtic (maybe inevitably) then went on to win. Fans of a certain age never tire of recalling that particular free kick and goal.

Great player, great times!

58

Frank McGarvey and Davie Provan hold aloft the Scottish Cup
in 1985 after defeating Dundee United in the final.

IT'S A MATTER OF CELTIC FACT

After winning six Scottish Cup medals with the club, Celtic legend JIMMY McMENEMY added another to his collection in 1921 when he was a member of the Partick Thistle team that defeated Rangers 1-0 in the final. The inside-forward was just a young forty-years-old at the time!

When HENRIK LARSSON made his first Celtic appearance (as a substitute for German striker Andy Thom in the opening game of Season 1997/98 at Easter Road), his misplaced pass found Chic Charnley who then scored what proved to be Hibernian's winning goal.

In 1953, during an encounter with Aberdeen at Celtic Park, playmaker BOBBY COLLINS (often 'The Wee Barra' or sometimes 'The Pocket Dynamo') netted three penalty kicks for his side in the ninety minutes.

Everybody knows that Celtic won the EUROPEAN CUP in May 1967. It is also worth remembering that they were the first Scottish, first British and first non-Latin club to achieve this distinction. Additionally, it was Celtic's first attempt to win this trophy and they succeeded with players of just one nationality from the club's homeland which was another first.

So severe was the arm damage sustained by winger JIMMY DELANEY in an early 1939 game that amputation was a considered option. Thankfully this course of action was eventually ruled out but the player never wore the hoops for another twenty-eight months such was the severity of the injury. In due course, he joined Manchester United.

By lifting the SCOTTISH CUP in 1995, Celtic continued the '5' sequence of wins that began in 1965 and continued in 1975 and 1985. Roll on 2005!

Seemingly, it was Scotland team manager Tommy Docherty who coined the wonderful and appropriate nickname 'The Quiet Assassin' for legendary midfielder DAVID HAY who later managed Celtic to League and Cup success in the 1980s.

When Celtic won 3-0 at Ibrox in late April 2001, it was Rangers biggest OLD FIRM home defeat in thirty years. The subsequent 2-0 Celtic victory at the same location in September that year confirmed the fact a Celtic side had recorded their first back-to-back Govan victory in some seventeen years.

Slovak LUBO MORAVCIK delighted the Celtic Park faithful when, during an August 1999 league clash with Hearts, he audaciously both trapped and controlled the ball.....with his backside!

When King HENRIK LARSSON scored fifty-three times in Season 2000/01, he not only smashed Charlie Nicholas' eighteen-year-old post-war record of forty-eight goals in one season but also equalled Brian McClair's 1986/87 tally of thirty-five Premier League strikes. King of Goals, to say the least!

JACKIE McNAMARA (Players' Player of the Year for Season 1997/98) suffered a career-threatening injury back in March 1989 when he shattered his right leg in two places during a training session with juvenile side Edina Hibs in Edinburgh.

During the famed NINE-IN-A-ROW sequence of championships (from Season 1965/66 to Season 1973/74 inclusive), Celtic scored a grand total of 868 goals in 306 league encounters. On average, therefore, the team hit the back of the net 2.8 times per game throughout all of this period. Incidentally, not one of the nine titles was clinched at home although 1970/71 would have been but for reconstruction work at Celtic Park. The game was switched to Hampden.

In the 1960s, Lisbon Lion STEVE CHALMERS netted five times at the quarter-final stage of the League Cup tournament on two separate occasions. In Season 1964/65, it was a handful of goals for him when East Fife were beaten 6-0 and then, four years later, another high five came his way in the 10-0 destruction of Hamilton.

Celtic FANS were officially banned from Ibrox for the Old Firm encounter on the last day of April 1994. Although the visitors scored first (a deadly John Collins free-kick was met, not surprisingly, by a wall of silent sound), the game ended in a 1-1 draw. If Rangers had won that day, they would have clinched the league title in front of (only) their own supporters.

THE CORONATION CUP tournament of 1953 comprised the following top British clubs – Arsenal, Manchester United, Newcastle United and Tottenham Hotspur from England plus Celtic, Rangers, Hibernian and Aberdeen from Scotland. Celtic deposed of English champions Arsenal and Manchester United before beating Hibernian (earlier conquerors of both Tottenham and Newcastle) 2-0 in the Hampden final before a crowd of over 117,000.

Pre-First World War centre-forward JIMMY QUINN still holds a unique Old Firm record. During his Celtic career (1900-1915), the powerful goal man scored a hat-trick against Rangers a truly impressive FOUR times. One of those occasions was the Scottish Cup final of 1904 (the first-ever Scottish Cup final hat-trick) when he replaced Alec Bennett due to rumours that the Celtic centre was about to sign for Rangers. Four years later, he did indeed.

Full-back TOMMY GEMMELL netted the opener in both of Celtic's two European Cup finals. In the 1967 Inter Milan game, his second-half equaliser set Celtic on the road to the most famous of victories and then (in 1970) his scorching drive gave his team the lead against Feyenoord at the San Siro stadium in Milan.

IT'S A MATTER OF CELTIC FACT

HEADLINE NEWS
Answers

1. Petrov's two goals in the 4-1 Dunfermline win helps Celtic move to within just two points of leaders Rangers.
2. Celts progress in Europe after 2-1 away defeat to Celta Vigo.
3. Alan Thompson's penalty goal silences Ibrox.
4. Aberdeen 'keeper lets in seven goals at Celtic Park.
5. Celtic reach final of UEFA Cup after 1-0 victory in Oporto.
6. Scottish football's 'Mickey Mouse' tag surely bites the dust after Celtic 's stunning 2-0 Anfield triumph.
7. Victory in March 'Old Firm' game at Celtic Park.
8. Celtic so close to victory in the UEFA Cup final.
9. Blackburn Rovers are beaten 2-0 at Ewood Park in the UEFA Cup.
10. Alan Thompson's penalty goal against Hearts in the penultimate home game of the season keeps them at the top of the SPL.

MISSING WORD QUIZ
Answers

1. Douglas (with the score 0-0, Rab saves the Dundee striker's penalty-kick)
2. Johan (Mjallby's late winner in the March clash with Hibernian)
3. Hartson (John's fantastic Anfield goal in the UEFA Cup)
4. Petrov (Stilian's Easter Road winner on a night when both Larsson and Sutton are missing)
5. O'Neill's (First Old Firm defeat for Rangers under Alex McLeish)
6. Maloney (his performance and goal in the 3-1 defeat of Stuttgart)
7. Petrov (Stilian nets a double in the 4-1 Dunfermline win)
8. Thompson (Alan's penalty spot winner against Hearts in the penultimate SPL home game of the season)
9. Maloney (the youngster's double in the 6-2 crushing of Dundee)
10. Larsson (Henrik's double in the UEFA Cup final)

THE QUOTES QUIZ
Answers

1. Henrik Larsson after the UEFA Cup first-leg win over Blackburn Rovers.
2. Martin O'Neill referring to Porto's time wasting tactics in the UEFA Cup final.
3. Rab Douglas speaking about the prolonged CIS Cup penalty shoot-out with Partick Thistle.
4. Martin O'Neill speaking about Stilian Petrov after the player sustained a terrible mouth injury in the game with Livingston.
5. Henrik Larsson (The Herald, 26.10.02)
6. Neil Lennon after the March SPL victory over Rangers.
7. Shaun Maloney and first-team action.
8. Stilian Petrov on scoring against Stuttgart in the UEFA Cup and the birth of his son, also called Stilian.
9. Alan Thompson and Celtic's penalty opener at Ibrox in late April.
10. Chris Sutton after Celtic did their talking on the park in the Ewood Park UEFA Cup game with Blackburn Rovers.

CELTIC AND THE SCOTTISH/CIS CUPS QUIZ –
SEASON 2002/03
Answers

1. Inverness Caley Thistle were opponents on both occasions.
2. Shaun Maloney.
3. Paul Lambert.
4. 5-4 to Celtic.
5. Henrik Larsson.
6. First Division clubs St. Mirren and St. Johnstone were both beaten 3-0.
7. Stuttgart, Germany on UEFA Cup business.
8. John Hartson.
9. He snapped his left wrist.
10. Henrik Larsson, Neil Lennon and Joos Valgaeren.

SEASON 2002/03 OLD FIRM QUIZ
Answers

1. A 3-3 draw.
2. Henrik Larsson.
3. The 19-second goal was the fastest recorded in this traditional fixture.
4. It was John Hartson who came so close to scoring.
5. False – it was John Hartson.
6. Henrik Larsson.
7. Bobo Balde.
8. True – Mjallby was injured and Petrov was among the substitutes.
9. Jackie McNamara.
10. Alan Thompson and John Hartson.

CELTIC IN EUROPE QUIZ – SEASON 2002/03
Answers

1. FC Basel of Switzerland.
2. Momo Sylla.
3. 10-1.
4. 22.
5. He had now surpassed Ally McCoist's previous record of 21 European goals.
6. Chris Sutton.
7. Celtic had knocked a Spanish team out of Europe for the very first time.
8. Paul Lambert, Shaun Maloney and Stilian Petrov.
9. False – he had never previously been on a winning side there.
10. Chris Sutton.

CELTIC AND THE SPL QUIZ – SEASON 2002/03
Answers

1. Henrik Larsson and Stilian Petrov.
2. Dundee United (5-0, 17.8.02), Kilmarnock (5-0, 28.9.02) and Aberdeen (7-0, 3.11.02).
3. Joos Valgaeren.
4. John Hartson with 3 goals.
5. 6 times.
6. Aberdeen (10.8.02), Hearts (20.10.02), Dunfermline (27.10.02 and 3.5.03) and Kilmarnock (25.5.03).
7. False – he had also netted against Aberdeen in the second game of the season.
8. Stilian Petrov in the early May encounters with Dunfermline and Motherwell.
9. Alan Thompson from the penalty spot.
10. Alan Thompson and Shaun Maloney.

CELTIC TRUE? CELTIC FALSE?
Answers

1. True – the magnificent Glasgow Exhibition cup from 1902.
2. False – it was nearer 110 degrees!
3. False – the total is 38 times.
4. False – Season 1969/70 was the period in question.
5. True.
6. False – it was Gordon Durie of Rangers.
7. True.
8. False – it was thirty-two years.
9. True – he had won four consecutive medals with Rosenborg in Norway before joining Celtic in December 1997.
10. True – in the November 1964 clash with Barcelona in Spain.